NO PETS ALLOWED!

Chitra Soundar
Illustrated by Fay Austin

BLOOMSBURY EDUCATION

LONDON   OXFORD   NEW YORK   NEW DELHI   SYDNEY

BLOOMSBURY EDUCATION

Bloomsbury Publishing Plc

50 Bedford Square, London, WC1B 3DP, UK

29 Earlsfort Terrace, Dublin 2, Ireland

BLOOMSBURY, BLOOMSBURY EDUCATION and the Diana logo are trademarks of
Bloomsbury Publishing Plc

First published in Great Britain in 2023 by Bloomsbury Publishing Plc

Text copyright © Chitra Soundar, 2023

Illustrations copyright © Fay Austin, 2023

Chitra Soundar and Fay Austin have asserted their rights under the Copyright, Designs
and Patents Act, 1988, to be identified as Author and Illustrator of this work

A catalogue record for this book is available from the British Library

ISBN: PB: 978-1-80199-174-2; ePDF: 978-1-80199-172-8; ePub: 978-1-80199-171-1

2 4 6 8 10 9 7 5 3

Text design by Laura Neate

Printed and bound by CPI Group (UK) Ltd, Croydon, CR0 4YY

MIX
Paper | Supporting
responsible forestry
FSC® C013604

To find out more about our authors and books visit www.bloomsbury.com and sign up for
our newsletters

Contents

Chapter One

Keva Kailash loved helping out at Grandpa's pet adoption centre – Wild Friends. Grandpa rescued abandoned pets and looked after them until he placed them in loving homes. Before Grandpa opened Wild Friends, he used to be a travelling vet, looking after pets on cruises or animals that had to travel far to return to the wild.

Keva lived with Mum and
Grandpa in the flat above Wild
Friends. She helped out with chores
like cleaning cages and tanks,
writing name tags in English and
Latin and making fact sheets for
each of the animals.

Keva loved all
the animals that
were brought to
the centre – the
big ones, the small
ones, the long ones
and the short ones. She loved
pretty birds and ugly frogs. She
loved creatures that crawled and
those that swam. She loved critters,
crocs, beetles, bunnies, elephants,
giraffes... and the
list went on.
But the animal
she loved the
most was Atlas.

Atlas was not rescued and he
was definitely not up for adoption.
Atlas was Grandpa's pet tortoise.
Atlas was old. Very
old. Very, very
old. He was
ancient.

Fact sheet for Atlas

Class: Reptilia

Genus: manouria

Species: manouria emys

Common name: Asian Giant Tortoise

Favourite food:
- Lettuce
- Dandelions
- Bamboo

Favourite hobbies:
- Listening to Grandpa's stories about his life on the sea.
- Going on walks with Grandpa every day.

Best friends:
- Grandpa (and now Keva too).

Grandpa and Atlas had been together ever since Grandpa was a little boy. Atlas even had a passport and went with Grandpa on all his voyages. Even now when Grandpa went on holidays, Atlas went with him in a mobile home that Grandpa had made just for him.

Inside the mobile home there was a water fountain, a grassy patch, some rocks and stones to climb and a food bowl. Keva often brought some lettuce for Atlas before school when Grandpa was opening the centre. It was good that Atlas liked lettuce because Keva wasn't very fond of it.

Saturdays were the busiest days at Wild Friends. But one Saturday, when Keva ran into the centre with a big bag of lettuce for her animal friends, Grandpa had not opened the front doors yet. He was placing food into cups for each of the animals.

"Why haven't you opened the doors yet, Grandpa?"

"Ah, we're closed for the day," said Grandpa.

"But why?" asked Keva. She was hoping to hang out with Atlas and Grandpa.

Grandpa clucked his tongue. A lizard clucked back.

"I'm off to Cavendish General for the day," said Grandpa.

"What's that?" asked Keva.

Atlas looked up as if he too wanted to know.

"It's a hospital, Keva," said Grandpa. "Where doctors and nurses hustle and bustle doing stuff."

Keva opened and closed her mouth like Atlas did.

"Are you poorly?" she whispered.

"Not at all!" said Grandpa.

"Then why are you going there?"

"To get my MOT," said Grandpa.

"What's MOT?" asked Keva.

Atlas looked up again, as if he didn't know either.

"It's when the doctors test me from top to bottom to see if I'm good to run for a few more years," said Grandpa. "Now off you go and do whatever you do on Saturdays."

"I help out here," wailed Keva.

"Not today, my sweet," said Grandpa. "But if you want something to do, I have a job for you."

"Yes, please," Keva said quickly.

"Will you look after Atlas for me?" he asked. "I can't take him with me to the hospital."

That was very odd. Grandpa had never been without Atlas. But Keva was happy that Grandpa trusted her to look after Atlas.

"I'll take good care of him," said Keva, touching Atlas on his back.

Soon Grandpa went off to the hospital in a taxi. Keva and Mum waved to him. Atlas couldn't bear to watch. He stayed inside his shell.

Chapter Two

Keva was still worried about Grandpa. "Is Grandpa OK?" she asked Mum.

Mum put an arm around Keva. "Yes, Keva, the doctors will just do some tests on Grandpa to check if he's healthy."

"What tests?" asked Keva. "Spelling? Or maths? Or maybe geography, like the capital cities of the world?"

"Ah! Not that kind of test, Keva,"
said Mum with a chuckle. "They are
going to check whether Grandpa
can hear properly, see well and if his
heart is beating normally. Like how

18

Grandpa checks an animal when he rescues them."

"Do you think he will pass the tests?" Keva asked.

"With flying colours," said Mum. "Don't you worry!"

"Oh! When is my MOT?" asked Keva.

"Not for a while," said Mum. "If you eat your lettuce and don't give it to Atlas."

Keva giggled.

Back in her room, Keva read a story and Atlas listened. Keva sang a song and Atlas listened.

When Keva wanted to play hide
and seek, Atlas played too by hiding
in his shell.

Then Keva, Atlas and Mum had
an early lunch.

"I wonder if Grandpa is missing Atlas," said Keva, sharing a little piece of cucumber with Atlas.

"We can take Atlas with us when we bring Grandpa his lunch," said Mum, as she packed a lunch box.

"Really?"

"Yeah, your grandpa won't eat hospital food. Even for one afternoon," she said. "So I made some chapatis with vegetables and lentils for him."

"Did you hear that, Atlas?" said Keva. "You're going to see Grandpa inside the hospital."

Atlas looked up with a smile.

Keva brought out Atlas's mobile home and Atlas knew exactly what to do. He walked in through the special door and settled inside. Keva gave Atlas some raw radishes for the car journey. But the journey didn't take very long.

When Mum found a parking spot, Keva helped Atlas out of his mobile home. Then she slipped on his lead, just like Grandpa did, and led him towards the doors.

The hospital was big and busy. As Mum, Keva and Atlas went up the ramp, some people stopped to stare. *It's not every day that a tortoise walks into a hospital*, thought Keva.

As they came up to the entrance, the big glass double doors whooshed open. Atlas stopped.

"Don't be scared," whispered Keva. "I'm right here with you."

They followed Mum, turning this way and that way through a maze of corridors until they reached another big set of doors. *WHOOSH!*

Chapter Three

The double doors whooshed open and Mum walked into a big room with many beds, followed by Keva and Atlas.

Grandpa was in the last bed, furthest from the doors.

"Hey, Keva! Hey, Atlas!" Grandpa called.

"Grandpa?" asked Keva, peering through her glasses.

Grandpa looked different in a
blue hospital gown. She had never
seen him in anything other than a
flowery shirt and trousers.

Mum started setting out the
packed lunch on the side table. Keva
had to walk slowly so Atlas could
keep up. Before Keva and Atlas could

reach Grandpa's bed,
a voice boomed.

"Hey, you!"

The rude voice
startled Atlas and
he hid in his shell.

A surly man rushed into the
room with squeaky rubber shoes.

"Hey, you!" he shouted again.

Mum rushed to Keva's side and
stood in front of the man with her
hands raised.

"No turtles allowed in the
hospital," the man yelled at Mum.

Keva stepped out from behind
Mum.

"He's not a turtle," Keva said firmly. "He is *Manouria emys*, the Asian Giant Tortoise."

"That's right," said Grandpa from the bed, in his best TV narrator voice. "*Manouria emys* is the largest tortoise species in mainland Asia and considered the most primitive of living tortoises. The species resides in wet forest…"

The man interrupted Grandpa. "Then what is it doing in a hospital?"

Atlas retreated further into his shell.

"Because he is family," said Keva. "Tell him, Mum. Atlas is getting scared."

Mum stepped closer, towering over the man, and looked down and asked, "Who are you?"

"I'm Mr Sallow," yelled the man. "And I'm the hospital manager. I make the rules around here."

Then he pointed at the sign on the wall that said: **NO PETS ALLOWED!**

"Oh!" Mum moved back, looking at the sign.

"I want the turtle out of the premises right now," Mr Sallow yelled.

"He's a tortoise," screeched Keva. "An Asian Giant Tortoise!

Tell him Mum, Atlas is missing Grandpa."

Mum turned to Keva. "We have to obey hospital policy, sweetie," she said. "Even if we don't like it."

Keva's nose flared and her face flushed pink.

"I'm not going anywhere," she said. "Neither is Atlas."

Before Mum could reason with Keva, Mr Sallow spoke, this time in a quiet voice which was scarier than his loud voice. "If you don't go right now, young lady, I'll have to confiscate your turtle and give him away to the wildlife park."

Keva muttered angrily under her breath. "He's not a turtle! He's an Asian Giant Tortoise."

"Of course, Mr Sallow," said Mum sweetly. "But you see, your hospital food is terrible. The lumpy mash, watery peas and limp bread are definitely not fit for consumption. I brought a home-cooked lunch for my dad. Until he has finished eating, we're not going anywhere."

"You can stay," said Mr Sallow. "The turtle must go."

"The TORTOISE is not going anywhere," said Keva, loudly this time.

"It definitely is," said Mr Sallow, reaching for the lead.

Mr Sallow pulled.

"Hey! You'll hurt him."

"Wait, wait," said Mum, gently taking the lead in her hand. "Let's not make a scene. There must be another way to resolve this."

A nurse hurried over to them. "The girl and her pet can wait with me in the nurses' station," she said. Then she looked at Keva and added, "Hello, my name is Nurse Nicole, what's yours?"

"Keva."

"Thank you, Nurse Nicole," said Mum.

"Fine!" muttered Mr Sallow.

Mum whispered to Keva. "Stay out of trouble."

Grandpa gave Keva and Atlas a thumbs-up and a wave.

Nurse Nicole offered Keva a spinning chair next to hers. Atlas sat next to Keva's chair but stayed in his shell. *All of this must be scary for him*, thought Keva.

As Nurse Nicole got busy filling in forms and taking phone calls, Keva got bored. She walked around the little cubicle and peered through a glass window into an office. No one was in there.

"Come, Atlas," whispered Keva, so she wouldn't attract Nurse Nicole's attention. "Let's explore."

Atlas didn't move at first. Keva bent down and whispered again, "Come on!"

Atlas walked slowly behind Keva as she tiptoed into the office. The room was quite small. On one wall, there were photos of a boy and his family. On the opposite side, the wall was covered in framed photographs of Mr Sallow standing next to many different people. *Must be famous patients*, thought Keva, as she moved closer to look.

Suddenly a rude, familiar voice asked, "What are you doing in here?"

Chapter Four

Keva turned around to face Mr Sallow. The tiny office got quickly crowded with one angry manager, one angry girl and a scared Giant Asian Tortoise. Keva kneeled on the floor next to Atlas.

"Don't worry," she whispered. "We'll be leaving soon."

"I'm not worried," said Mr Sallow.

"I'm talking to Atlas," said Keva. "He is upset because you don't like him."

Atlas peeped out a tiny bit. Keva took out some lettuce leaves from her pocket and offered them to him. Atlas grabbed them with his mouth and retreated back into his shell.

"Go back to the nurses' station," said Mr Sallow. "I don't want *that* in my office."

"*That* is a living creature with feelings," said Keva.

TRING!

The phone rang and Mr Sallow sat at his desk to take the call.

Keva returned
to the wall of
photos. One photo
made her curious:
a young boy, who

looked like he must be Mr Sallow as
a child, holding a shell. Where had
she seen that shell pattern before,
she wondered.

Keva sprung up on her feet and
stood on tiptoes to take a closer look.
The younger Mr Sallow was not
holding just a shell. He was holding
an *Achatina fulica* – a Giant African
land snail. Keva wrote a fact sheet
for one just last week, when Grandpa
had arrived with his latest rescue.

"That's a Giant African land snail," said Keva, turning to Mr Sallow, who was now staring at her from behind the desk. "*Achatina fulica*! Did he have a name?"

"Solomon," whispered Mr Sallow, putting the phone down.

"Did you know these snails can smell their owners and recognise them?" asked Keva, bending to pat Atlas on the head and feed him more lettuce.

Atlas munched and Mr Sallow replied, "It would have been useful if they could smell predators."

"Why, what happened?"

Mr Sallow reclined on his chair and stared at the ceiling. "It was a summer's day. A weekend."

"Saturday or Sunday?" asked Keva.

"A Saturday for sure! I remember well," replied Mr Sallow. "Solomon sat by the window sill watching the world go by. He liked to do that a lot."

"Then?" said Keva.

"My brother came into the room with Denzel."

"Who is Denzel?"

"My brother's Giant Asian Tortoise," said Mr Sallow. "Like that one."

"That's Atlas," said Keva.

Atlas looked up, recognising his name.

"My brother put Denzel on the sideboard next to the window," continued Mr Sallow. "At first I didn't think anything of it. But then, as we began to play our board game, Denzel the tortoise slowly moved towards Solomon."

"To sit with Solomon?"

"No," barked Mr Sallow. "Denzel wanted to eat my Solomon. I could see him licking his lips."

"That can't be true," said Keva. Atlas practically lived in an animal rescue centre and he had never attempted to eat any other creature.

"I know what I saw," said Mr Sallow. "One minute Denzel was on the sideboard, and the next minute, he was at the window sill munching on Solomon's lettuce. Solomon had disappeared."

"Oh!" said Keva. "Giant Asian Tortoises definitely don't eat Giant African land snails! Maybe Denzel just wanted to eat lettuce? I bet Solomon fell into the garden and disappeared into the bushes. Did you check in the garden?"

Mr Sallow snapped up straight in his chair. "What?" he barked.

Startled, Atlas looked up.

"You didn't check?" demanded Keva. "Poor Solomon must have been wandering in the garden, lost and alone."

Mr Sallow's face suddenly softened. It dawned on him that maybe Denzel hadn't eaten Solomon after all. "Oh no!" he cried. "What have I done?"

"It's too late for Solomon now," said Keva. "Giant African land snails only live up to nine or ten years."

"And all those years he might have been looking for me," said Mr Sallow, sadly.

"What happened then?"

"I made my parents give him to the local wildlife park," said Mr Sallow.

"Your brother?"

"No! His tortoise, Denzel," replied Mr Sallow.

"You owe him an apology," said Keva.

"To my brother?"

"And to Denzel," she reminded him. "I'm sure he'll still be in the wildlife park. Tortoises can live up to 100 years."

Mr Sallow sighed and closed his eyes.

Chapter Five

When they reached home, Keva
settled Atlas back in his spot behind
the counter. She was thinking
about how much Mr Sallow must
have loved Solomon for him to be
annoyed with tortoises so many years
later. *Maybe I can help Mr Sallow,*
Keva thought.

"We have to go back to the
hospital to get Grandpa in an hour

or so," said Mum, walking upstairs. "I hope we don't run into that ghastly man again."

But Keva was hoping to run into Mr Sallow. She had a plan and it started right there at Wild Friends. Keva opened Grandpa's animal register. She scanned the list, her fingers tracing the Latin names down the page.

"There!" she cried. "Home 3."

Atlas peeped out of his shell to see why Keva was excited.

Keva located the shelf marked Home 3. She peeped inside the large glass tank on the shelf and smiled.

"Perfect," she whispered, dropping some lettuce leaves into the tank.

Then she opened Grandpa's encyclopedia to the page titled 'Giant African land snail'. Then, just as Grandpa always did, she made a care sheet.

Everything was ready for her
visit to the hospital. "This will work,
Atlas," said Keva.

Atlas looked up without a smile.

As if on cue, Mum called, "Time
to go, Keva!"

Mum brought Atlas out in his
mobile home and placed him in the

back seat of the car. Keva climbed
in next to Atlas carrying a box.

"What's that?" asked Mum.

"A surprise!" said Keva.

*

Grandpa was waiting for them by the big double doors. Mum got out of the car and waved to Grandpa. Keva rushed to Grandpa's side with her box.

"Hello, Keva," said Grandpa. "What's that?"

"A surprise," said Keva.

"For me?" he asked.

"Nope!" said Keva. "For Mr Sallow."

Grandpa frowned. "Mr Sallow was rude, but that doesn't mean we have to give him any rude surprises, my lovely," he said.

"Come on, Grandpa," said Keva. "It's not a rude surprise, I promise."

Keva marched through the swishing double doors and straight into Mr Sallow's office, closely followed by Grandpa.

Mr Sallow looked up and grumbled, "What now?"

"This is for you, Mr Sallow," said Keva with a smile, placing the box on the table.

"What's that?" he barked.

"It's a surprise," said Grandpa in a flat voice, making Keva giggle.

"I don't like surprises," said Mr Sallow.

"I don't blame you," said Grandpa. "This one might be rude. You've been warned," he muttered.

"It's not, Grandpa," said Keva. "Open it, Mr Sallow."

"I wouldn't," said Grandpa.

"I'm not scared," mumbled
Mr Sallow as he pulled the box
closer and opened it.

Mr Sallow let out a loud gasp.

"What is the surprise?" asked
Grandpa.

"Solomon," Mr Sallow mumbled.

"Who's Solomon?" asked Grandpa.

"He's not your old friend Solomon, Mr Sallow," said Keva. "But he is a new friend. Maybe he could be called Solomon the Second?"

Mr Sallow smiled and his eyes filled with tears. "Thank you," he gushed.

All day, Keva had only seen Mr Sallow's frown. Now he was smiling and crying all at the same time.

Grandpa peeped inside the box and gasped. "*Achatina fulica,*" he said.

"Yup! Are you OK for Mr Sallow to look after him, Grandpa?"

"Are you sure?" asked Grandpa. "What if he doesn't know how to take care of him?"

"I made a
care sheet,"
said Keva,
handing the sheet
to Mr Sallow.

"Call me if
you need help
looking after him,"
said Grandpa. "Don't
let Keva down."

"I'll take good care of Solomon
the Second," said Mr Sallow.
"Thank you both."

The double doors whooshed
open again and Grandpa waved to
Mum and Atlas in the car park. As

Keva stepped outside, a pleasant voice called, "Keva!"

Mr Sallow was sprinting towards them with a sign in his hands and a smile on his face.

"Maybe he doesn't want the snail?" muttered Grandpa.

"He loves that snail, I'm sure of it," said Keva.

Keva was right. Mr Sallow was not returning Solomon the Second. He had something else to share.

"I took down the 'No Pets Allowed' sign," said Mr Sallow, "I'm going to invite animals into the hospital to cheer people up."

Keva clapped her hands and jumped up and down like a bouncing ball. "Yay! Thanks, Mr Sallow!"

"Thank *you* for everything," said Mr Sallow with more tears in his eyes.

"What's going on?" asked Mum, walking over to them with Atlas.

Keva told Mum and Grandpa about how she had found out about Mr Sallow's pet snail Solomon and about Denzel.

"Then?" asked Mum.

"Then, I brought him Solomon the Second from Wild Friends."

"Oh, that was the box of surprise!" said Mum.

"Thanks to Keva, I'm going to visit Denzel the tortoise in the wildlife park," said Mr Sallow. "And ask for his forgiveness too."

After Mr Sallow went back in the hospital, Grandpa pulled Keva into a big hug. "I'm so proud of you, Keva," he said. "You've returned Mr Sallow's rudeness with your kindness."

"And now Mr Sallow has passed on the kindness to everyone in the hospital," said Keva. "Isn't that great, Atlas?" she asked. Atlas looked up and nodded.

Just for Fun

Keva's Joke Sheet

No tortoises or snails were harmed in the making of these jokes.

1. How did the snail feel when he fell off the tree?

Shell-shocked.

2. How do tortoises hide from predators?

They keep a slow profile.

3. Why are snail shells so shiny?

They use snail varnish.

4. When a young tortoise misbehaves, what does their mum say?

Go to your shell.

5. Why are snails always caught after a crime?

They leave a trail.

READING ZONE!

GET CREATIVE

Look at the care sheet that Keva wrote on page 51. Choose your own animal to research, and then write a care sheet that could be given to a customer if they took the animal home as a pet.